MW01520173

Dumitru C Ciobanu, author of *The Eyes Are the Soul Mirror,* is a family man, a husband, and father of two beautiful children. Ever since childhood, he has been writing short stories and poems. It was a live-changing experience 13 years ago when he moved to London, but he never forgot the lessons life taught him, and he put in writing. *The Eyes Are the Soul Mirror* is a book that he hopes you will enjoy. Together, we are stronger.

To my grandmother, Florica.

Dumitru C Ciobanu

THE EYES ARE THE SOUL MIRROR

AUSTIN MACAULEY PUBLISHERS™

LONDON • CAMBRIDGE • NEW YORK • SHARJAH

Copyright © Dumitru C Ciobanu 2024

The right of Dumitru C Ciobanu to be identified as author of this work has been asserted by the author in accordance with sections 77 and 78 of the Copyright, Designs and Patents Act 1988.

All rights reserved. No part of this publication may be reproduced, stored in a retrieval system, or transmitted in any form or by any means, electronic, mechanical, photocopying, recording, or otherwise, without the prior permission of the publishers.

Any person who commits any unauthorised act in relation to this publication may be liable to criminal prosecution and civil claims for damages.

This is a work of fiction. Names, characters, businesses, places, events, locales, and incidents are either the products of the author's imagination or used in a fictitious manner. Any resemblance to actual persons, living or dead, or actual events is purely coincidental.

A CIP catalogue record for this title is available from the British Library.

ISBN 9781035827107 (Paperback)
ISBN 9781035827114 (Hardback)
ISBN 9781035827121 (ePub-e-book)

www.austinmacauley.com

First Published 2024
Austin Macauley Publishers Ltd®
1 Canada Square
Canary Wharf
London
E14 5AA

Introduction

There in the world are different speculations to the view of things. We have the good and the bad. Most of the time, the good part of life is always subject to the bad side of life. The bad attacks the good and leaves it helpless. This makes a lot of people seek that which is bad because most times bad wins in the battle.

In a generation where people want to see the exploitation of miracles, they know the good can take so much time so they would just have to go to the bad to get it very quickly. The good can take ten years for what the person wants to do. Moving to the bad, in just a jiffy the work is done and the task is met.

"The battle line of good and bad runs through the heart of every man."

Aleksandr Solzhenitsyn

These have evolved through the present man; it has now in fact sprung up in the life of today. The bad ruling over the good. The bad has dominion over the good. The bad enjoy life while the good is a servant to life.

Anyways, this can go on for years, but after some moments the good would still always rule. It might be a long time but it will get back his dominion and put the bad in their bad position.

If you don't understand this, join me as I take us on a memory lane of the history between good and bad. The personality of the good and the personality of the bad. The trials they went through and the endpoint; how the bad overcame the good and how the good eventually came into being.

Here is a story of a personality subject to another personality. It's a historical story that will bring a message to all. Be attentive to the words and be sure to get the real picture behind the story and the main essence of the story.

Happy reading …

The Beginning

It all started in the beginning.

A world was created. This world was stipulated and things were done according to the ruler; God. Everywhere was metaphysical and there was no breed to life. It existed just on its own. The darkness went through the face of the world and all situation was hopeless. The creator of the world came and made the world. A ruler like no other is seen making things out of nothing. The world is still amazed at how wonderfully he could do, all he did, in the best of way.

Vegetation was made, it wasn't enough. Seas were flowing, which spread through the world yet it was still not enough. What of the creatures that existed lowly? They were created but it was still not enough. Something was missing. These creatures couldn't exist alone without something or someone in charge of it. It was at this point the ruler decided to create a man.

Man is created; there was a delight in the world yet it was just a man. Not all were created at the same time. It started with the man called Adam. The first man of creation was this man by the name Adam. There were angels who were on deck to create this being of a man. He lived his early life taking charge of the whole things in the world. Just a man was in charge of the whole mystery that existed in life. He was doing it alright but he was just the only one of his being. He needed a shoulder to lean on.

Most times, he played with the trees as he saw the trees pollinate each other. These were sweet times for him, he also saw the animals mate each other. Wow! He was so amazed and wished he could have that kind of a sweet life.

The ruler heard his thought and together in a short moment another being came to the world. This was really another being because it was a woman. She was very different from the man. As she was created, she began to grow and on a day the ruler took her to the man he has created.

Immediately, Adam saw her, his eyes were in a moment of shock. He couldn't imagine anything less as he never thought another creature of his kind could exist. In the joy of the moment, he held unto her arms and called her Eve. He was so joyous and she was also. With that, he wasn't anymore lonely.

He went to places with his Eve, who had now become his wife.

The ruler came to see the man he had created and the one who was his lover. They were such of a beauty and he was so happy they merged each other. As they were new to the standard of the world as no world remained at that time, he began to teach them all things. He communicated with them as a father to children. The love he had for them was so much. In the day and in the night, he made their company his abode and they enjoyed their time with him.

There was nothing like looking for food so he had to show him where his food was. For the firstborn of creation, they shouldn't lack anything; should they?

He showed unto him things he was to do but it was all in affluence. The ruler really loved his creature that he provided him with everything; he and his wife. But, he knew it wasn't enough for him to just have everything, so he gave him a threshold to things.

The ruler had to put a boundary for him in the food he was to eat. He knew how much his man loved food but he wouldn't want him to always live by everything. For a being that hopes to live forever in the hands of his master, he must be ready to follow certain rules. He needed to have allergy for a particular food. Every other food was available but for a particular food, he and his wife were not to go anywhere near it. The ruler told them in one of their conversations. Adam heard the ruler say that and he asked no further question. He continued with the works for the day.

The woman; Eve was still new to the surrounding. The world was so large that she needed to check through everywhere. She could never imagine how the world could look so beautiful so she kept checking around the globe. She saw all the beautiful creatures and was intrigued by how they looked. At that time, Adam was busy watching over the trees and the seas. He didn't know his woman had gone around the world. She also didn't know where her Adam was. She wanted to procreate many children as she also saw the other creatures do so but she had no sight of him and how to do it.

In the interim, as she was considering each of their uniqueness, one of the creatures; the snake saw her and decided to have a conversation with her. She couldn't understand how it already knew a lot about her. The snake involved her in a long conversation even as she began to forget her Adam. She was so intrigued by its conservation.

She was there with the snake for a long time and with its sweet talks she sat to listen. Sighing that she has gotten the attention of the snake, it soon started up by asking her some personal questions she was gullible about.

She entertained the snake and the snake noticed she didn't take a particular food. She was the second person in the world so why would she not consume a particular food. It pressurized her into knowing the exact truth. She finally told it the hidden truth. She was being so good to the creature of her creator and she was also naive. She had no thought of tomorrow as today looked so pleasant to her.

She told him of the boundaries her creator had set for she and her husband. Either or not it was true, she was ready to follow the instructions to the end but she knew not the reason. The snake was being a bad one by influencing the good one to do that which was wrong to their creator.

He persuaded her to believe the wrong truth and she became reconcilable. The woman saw for herself that the food might not be allergic to her, so she ate the food and saw how delicious the food was to her belly. She couldn't enjoy the food alone, so when the snake was off hearing as they were done with the conversation; she began to look for her husband again.

Finally, she found him, prepared the food and gave it to him. Immediately, he saw the food, he recognized it as the food the ruler had told them not to eat.

"Eve, this is but the food our creator told us not to eat," Adam said as he was puzzled.

"Not so, dear. This food isn't our allergy, taste it, it tastes so delicious," Eve said as she gave it to him.

That was the love of his life giving him a delicious food after he was back from his stress less work. He didn't ask too many questions as she gave him all necessary answers before he could be ready to question the details.

He didn't hesitate even as he began to eat the delicious food and paying less attention to the words from the ruler. The food was so delicious and they continued eating it. After some minutes, they began to admire each other and noticed some things had changed about them. They became timid of each other.

It was at this time, the ruler came. Times before whenever he came, they would have been waiting for him at a certain position but this time, he didn't see them there. The ruler already knew what they had done. He was tense as he saw his creation, hide themselves as they saw him. He couldn't just calm down to hear any of their excuses because they kept shifting blames on each other.

How? Why? When?

Those were questions rooting out from the ruler yet the man was so confused and he felt disappointed for his vulnerable acts.

"How can you be so greedy? I gave you everything life could give to humanity, just a boundary and you couldn't just live by it," the ruler said in fury.

"I am so sorry, Master. I forgot," Adam said and it got the ruler more pissed off.

"You forgot! How can the firstborn of creation forget things so easily? Couldn't you just live in my shadow for a while?" The ruler asked not backing out but Adam and Eve had nothing to say.

They stood there scared of what might happen. God could not be pacified. They could not live in the same place as he was living. Their existence meant nothing to him anymore. He ordered his newly created messenger to have the ones he has created maimed. Adam and Eve cried but there was none to save them.

In a split second, their body was gone.

The man that was created was created with his body and soul. Since his body was the physical part that went down to death, the soul cannot be put to death. Their soul had to be kept somewhere for a specific time being.

Trees were the other source of dominion at that time, so their soul was shut up in the trees of life forever.

The world was empty just so again and God; the ruler couldn't just procreate life in the belly of the beast so he created other new Adams and Eves. They eventually spread throughout the earth.

God had to reproduce his first kind of creation so he sent their soul after into the body of different animals. Man came out as a new identity in animals.

Their soul began to dwell in the body of animals like the pig, bird, rabbit and lion.

In a space of a time, the world began to change. Everything got a new shape. The Adams spread through the earth and the generation of Eve spread. Life had to begin again and there was a need for love to dwell and for there to be indifferences. People became very much different from the other person as languages began to differentiate everyone. In different nations and constituents did they begin to exist.

There had to be a way of buying and selling things so God made money in its different currency to meet with the demands of man. The Pandora box was also made within that period as a source of trouble that wouldn't be made known to humanity. Before any evil would happen, God would have already known about that so he would shield the person from such danger.

God was the good expression to mankind. He changed humanity for man's sake. They became more and more in the earth as they began to procreate. Each of them giving birth to male and female. It was so amazing how two people became billions of people in the universe.

The world was stable but then, there came an enemy.

The enemy has been bound by God for a long time but he still surfaced each time to do a bad act. Nothing good ever came out of him. The enemy was the devil!

As good as God was to the earth, the devil was the bad expression to the earth. He transcended from the snake that lured the woman to the serpent that attacked the universe. The devil is never satisfied with his evil schemes so he continues through the whole generation doing many bad acts in the face of time.

God so good had a lot of good angels who he sent out frequently to attend to the need of his people. The devil being an imitator of life also had his own bad angels. He was able to dissuade some of God's angels from the truth and bring them to his own stead. Both the good and bad angels were all messengers. The work they did was just the difference.

God gave his people a good angel to meet with their daily demands and the devil gave the angels a chance to attack man in high esteem. The best way to effect a change in humanity is from the womb of a woman. This became his source of inspiration. Whenever a woman gets pregnant, the devil sends his angels to put in his offspring in the belly of that woman or sometimes for him to kill the child.

As God was producing his offspring through the belly of the woman, the devil was producing his own offspring. So, we have in the world children that are representations of the devil. It was in it's vast world even as this offspring's began to bruise over each other.

The children of God who were the good ones were in most times attacked by the children of the devil. The devil could not dwell everywhere so his offspring represented him everywhere. When a child dies, it can be traced to the devil. He wasn't just allowing the children of God to live for so long without him tormenting them.

There are cases of attacks on the children of God. When a child of God is doing good and helping humanity, the child of the devil would come to frustrate his act. He could come by inflicting the child with various kind of illness. Children of God were finding it difficult to live without his torment. It was just some of them who had dominion over these bad children but that was in a smaller quantity.

The ruler of the universe couldn't just stay in his chamber and watch his offspring be under the subjection of this evil being. Right from his mighty throne, he sends judgement to attack these evil men and sets his children free from their grip. It has always been a battle exceeding from year to year. God never fails in any of the battle but most times his children are always in deep pains for the affliction that have come to them.

This wouldn't have happened if the first Adam hasn't had a representation of evil in him. It is as a result of these evil practice the first Adam did, that the other Adams were suffering. As descendants of Adam, they have inherited his mistakes and vulnerabilities. This made it easy for the devil to attack them fast. To him, they cannot be smarter than their early father and mother who he tempted and won over.

Year went after year and the devil wasn't stopping. His threat was over the house of God as he kept tormenting them. Man was not pulling out through because his schemes were very funny and fast. He had the scheme of manipulating things without man knowing anything about it. The devil has his powers that he uses to afflict man and this was in all his agents, but the children of God didn't have so much power because they have given into fear and wouldn't just let the master have his way over them.

Meanwhile, their main weakness was because they couldn't see! The devil and his host could see through any human and begin to attack them but for the children of God, their sight was limited. They couldn't see through the soul of man to know which of them was actually a child of God or the child of the devil. With this inability to see, they were always attacked.

They were really helpless and that continued in the earth for several centuries.

After several centuries, the king of the earth had to do something quick, else the devil would keep reigning without looking back.

God needed to pull a strategy that would eventually put this devil in his rightful place. God as good, has been on the battle with the devil as bad, for many centuries. So, there had to be a plan. It was a divine strategy known only to God and his host. It was to be a hidden operation that wouldn't be known to the devil and any of his hosts. The devil wouldn't always have his ways. Good must always glory over the bad.

A new creation was born into the world!

This wasn't a creature like every other, this was a special creature born into the world. He was a special being with a physical body. The mystery behind his birth wasn't so well known to people. All that was known was that he had a grandma who was in charge of taking of care of him. No thought of his parents just his grannie.

This grandma was sent by God to preserve this child. She treated him as her own. He grew up bearing the name; Hi because nobody actually knew his name. He was so new to the setting of the world system and how everything operated. He heaved a sigh as he saw the trees and seas in the earth. He and his grandma began to grow in a small region of the world.

This boy was a gentle and a smart one. He started up his life doing what was right in the sight of people. He was living all right. As a young child, he stayed with his grandma and followed her every instruction. He was trained with a lion heart and did so well. He never told a lie and didn't in fact engage in any bad act. When every other person of his age kept doing all sort of inordinacies, he maintained his calm demeanour. Helping his granny with a lot of work and keeping a close check on people. He enjoyed speaking with people of his class and higher than him. Knowledge was his key.

There was no evil to be traced to him as he lived life as a saint.

Grandma couldn't understand how a fine young child could be so equipped with that kind of knowledge of right or wrong. She saw to herself that the name; Hi doesn't in anyway match his speculation. She couldn't sit back and watch people call him that. She checked for his birth certificate in some old briefcase and while she saw it, she changed his name to Demetrius, since he was like a saint. She also called him Constantin like the saint.

This began to sound very nice to the ears of the people. Some had to call him by a short form of Deme and it sounded really nice to his ears. He had a few close friends and they had good times together. Whenever they went out, he always acted ahead of everyone because he was really ahead of them in everything.

He began to grow in an unusual way, and while he was nine years of age, the grandma noticed in his mouth, a tooth growing at the centre. Why would a teeth be growing at the centre of his mouth, she couldn't just place her hand on it?

The granny was so scared because he had never been sick since he was born. She couldn't understand the growth in his teeth. She was scared that he was going to die so she went to every place where she could get healing for him.

She came back with the medicine that day, but found out the teeth had grown into a good shape. She was amazed at such a miracle but most especially delighted that he had gotten much better. She held him closely and told him never to fall ill again. He just smiled and continued with the work he was doing that day. It was just a growth, not an illness so he wasn't to be bothered.

He continued doing what he was doing and in his school, this boy was the best in everything he did. Every other person came after him. The way and the manner he excelled in everything he did was of immense concern to each of his mates but there was nothing they could do about that. He was the most intelligent guy in the class. It didn't matter if it were science courses, commercial courses or art courses, he excelled in it all. A child like no other. From elementary classes, he was already solving the work of senior classes. He was a person who was sought after. His seniors took him like their senior because he knew more than them. Each time there was a competition in school they would always scream; Demetrius.

All of his tutors were really so privileged to have him as their student. They sometimes took the glory by thinking to their selves that they were the ones who had taught him into excellence. Everyone likes to be linked to good things so this was the case with his teachers. They really loved him so much and were proud of him.

He was really so intelligent and he was the nicest person to talk to. He related well with everyone in his school. There was no dull moment with him. He taught people to do what was right and really helped them in keeping to their dreams. He hated hearing people talk about failure as he believed failure could be worked upon, so whenever any academically poor student came to him, he rendered the help he could give to them, to make them up to the mark.

Everyone would hold unto him and call him their favourite. Demetrius would just always smile as he knew his intelligent quotient wasn't from the natural realm but from the spiritual realm. It wasn't just that, the creator of life was in creator, so what's their expectation? Where they expecting him to be behind, that could never happen.

It wasn't just in school works that he did so well, in extracurricular activities he did extremely well. He enjoyed sporting activities so much that he was involved in all the sporting activities that was to be done in the school and in the city at large. He had in fact won a medal as the fastest athlete in the city. Meanwhile, his favourite of all of the sport was football. Once the ball hit his leg it was so sure of hitting the net. There was no error!

All hit and a goal. His team was the best because of him. He had the best coach but he was the reason their team did so well. He was the captain of his team.

There was a competition between his school and one of the best schools in the city at that time. Those guys had never lost any football match before, so when they heard there was a good footballer in a nearby school, they decided to engage them in a football match.

Immediately, the news got through Demetrius' school, they had mixed feelings. First, they were scared of this school and on the other hand they were delighted they had Demetrius in their team, so it was a competition between good and good. They had to start preparing well for the competition. Throughout the day and the next day, it was all about the football match.

Meanwhile, the devil at another end was observing this guy; Demetrius. Anyone who was growing in an exceptional way in the kingdom calls for the devil attention. As he saw him, he began to observe each of the things he was doing. The devil was so shocked to see Demetrius had been so excellent in all that he did.

"What do you think of this boy called Demetrius," the devil asked his angel as they were all looking at him.

"He isn't some normal creature. I have tried attacking him but there is this wall of defence around him which I don't understand," one of the angels of the devil said and the devil laughed hysterically.

"Wall of defence!" the devil said as he laughed. "Any defence is either coming from our side or from the highest so he must be getting some protection from the angels of God since we aren't at his defence," the devil said, laughing.

"Give your command and we would do the needful," another angel said, bowing his head to the devil.

"What are they doing here?" the devil asked, still laughing.

"They all preparing for a football match, tomorrow," his angel said.

"Then, I would be here tomorrow to see him," the devil said, laughing even as they all went.

As they went, Demetrius looked towards the back and saw them moving. He was the only one who had the eyes to see through both physical beings and spiritual beings. He smiled as he saw them leave. He didn't know what to do but he just continued in his preparation.

The match commenced on a Friday afternoon. All team were on deck as they came to the field. Both teams began to greet each other as they headed to the field.

"Captain, that's their best player," the coach of Demetrius team said, as he pointed to a bow legged young boy.

"That's no problem, sir. We wouldn't have to meet. I will be at their striker's end and he would be at our striker's end. No interference!"

Demetrius smiled as he ran into the field.

The contests started as the referee blew the whistle.

It was strike through, strike out. Defence was so tight. The other team started out well, they were with high ball possession, they were just with the ball for the first 15 minutes. The ball wasn't just getting to the legs of Demetrius' team. They struggled through that time to get the ball.

But after about 17 minutes, Andrew; a midfielder collected the ball from the other team. As he collected the ball, there was a loud noise in the pitch. He began to dribble through the ball and he finally passed the ball to Peter; a good striker but Peter could not control the ball from his end else it would be an offside play, so he immediately passed the ball to Demetrius and immediately Demetrius got the ball, it was a direct goal to the net.

The whole pitch was in a loud noise as Demetrius scored the goal. The other team were so surprised as to how he scored the goal immediately as his legs touched the ball. They continued in the match after some minutes of rejoicing. The other team continued playing as they tried to score, after about 20 minutes they scored their own goal making it 1–1.

At the time the football match was going on, some men at a particular spot kept observing Demetrius and the confidence he was showing at the battlefield. They were so proud of the moves he was making at the football match. The other team's coach kept controlling the whole match as he kept tailing them to remain with the ball. They continued with the high ball possession. All the sycophants on the field kept hailing Demetrius, and the bow legged boy of the other team.

Demetrius team finally got the ball again and the pass began. This time, it was James that passed the ball to Peter. Peter continued controlling the ball and just as he was about to pass the ball to Demetrius to score the final goal, the devil came in!

The devil wasn't seen by anyone in the football pitch. He came in like a wind. He sighted Demetrius as he played the ball on the field, he began to walk quietly from the back stage to the field, he kept walking directly to where Demetrius was. As Demetrius was about to get the ball to hit towards the goal, the devil came to where he was. Demetrius looked up and saw the devil.

The Devil

"Deme, hit the ball fast!" Peter screamed out to Demetrius.

Demetrius was with the ball when he saw the devil coming right to where he was. He stood with the ball under his leg; shocked at the mysterious being before him. He noticed that the person coming was not a normal being because if he was, he wouldn't be coming directly into the field without being stopped by the referee or somebody. He saw the way everything was going in the field; no one was looking at the direction of the devil, he wasn't seen by any other person except from Demetrius.

He stood there staring blankly at the devil as he came quietly to his side. While that was done, the other team collected the ball from him. They saw it as an opportunity to quickly head to the other end to score a goal.

The whole team of Demetrius was in disarray as they could not fathom how Demetrius simply lost that chance to score a goal. What was it he saw that made him stand still, they all wondered as he was still standing at the same spot confused. His coach noticed this and thought maybe he was sick from something. Since he had been the best all along, they could cut him some slack for that moment. Owing to that, from behind, the coach told another player to get substituted for him as they could not understand what went wrong. That looked like the best thing to do.

Demetrius still maintained the same posture as he was looking at the devil circumspective. The devil didn't in fact do anything, he just kept laughing at him trying to make him confused. The coach at that time signalled for Demetrius to be substituted as the other player was getting ready to take his place.

Demetrius was not ready to be defeated and he didn't seem scared of the devil. He signalled back to the coach that he was alright and there was no need for the substitution. The coach didn't know what to do, he was their best player so of course they needed him to focus and hit the goal. They all hoped for the best so he continued in the match not minding the mysterious being who was still standing out there looking at him hopelessly.

The match continued with the other team in ball possession. Just some minutes to the end of the match, Andrew got the ball and passed it directly to Peter. Peter wasn't in the position to score the goal because there were three players at his side trying to collect the ball from him. Peter at that point passed the ball to Demetrius. Demetrius collected the ball, looked at the devil to be sure there was no negative move, the devil also stared at him wondering where the courage was coming from as he could see him being so resilient.

Demetrius collected the ball and in the split of a second, he hit the ball at the net and that was a massive goal!

Wow! The other team was surprised. Two goals from the same person.

Everyone in his team came to where he was, to rejoice with him, they were so happy it was already 2–0. His coach smiled at him, happy that there was nothing wrong with him.

As they were rejoicing, the devil was in fury. He couldn't understand how he could score the goal when he was there watching him. He came up to where Demetrius was as he was still rejoicing with his team. The devil broadened his eyes towards Demetrius' legs and immediately Demetrius fell to the ground. The guys thought it was another way of him rejoicing not until he started calling for help did they know he was in real agony. He kept shouting at the top of his voice. His team players were so confused so they kept on asking him different questions as to the pain;

"Is it a muscle pull?"

"We need an aid here!"

"Deme, are you alright?"

"What's the problem with your leg!"

"Please, someone should come over here!"

The coach and his team players kept asking him simultaneously while he kept on shouting with the pain in his leg. He was taken out of the ball pitch as the nurse of the school began to check his leg out to give him necessary treatments. The devil was following him as they were carrying him to the hospital.

"Just take me home, please," Demetrius said to the nurse as she struggled to find out what was wrong.

"Just calm down, you would be alright," the nurse said trying to apply some ointment to the leg.

"Take me home, please. My treatment is at home," he said and the people with him tried to understand what happened to his legs and what he meant by; the treatment is at home.

The nurse couldn't see anything wrong in his legs as it looked completely fine. He was the only one feeling the pain and just the only one who knew where the problem was from.

He saw the devil singing some pathetic songs in the air. He didn't know why he was singing that but he was just not ready to create a scene. No one could see the devil so he had to just act like he wasn't seeing him.

"I have to go home now!" Demetrius said as he took his trainers with his bags heading directly home.

He kept holding on to his leg as he was heading out of the football field hastily. He kept falling and rising up.

The nurse and the coach could not stop him from going as they were all bewildered at what just happened. The nurse volunteered to escort him to his house as she could not leave him going home all by himself with that grievous pain.

"I will be fine. The other guys will need you. One of them might fall off, you should stand to protect them," Demetrius said still holding on to the pain in his leg.

He didn't want the devil to harm the other guys so he wouldn't have her go with him despite her persuasion.

"Alright, if you insist, just get home safe and rest properly after your treatment. I will watch over the other guys so you don't have to worry about them," the nurse said emphatically.

"Thank you so much, I really appreciate it," Demetrius said as he left the field, helplessly.

In the interim, the other team struggled to get another goal when the break was over. It remained ten minutes to the end of the match. Demetrius team was all for defence, they didn't even bother to strike anymore. The ten minutes finally ended and till the very end they scored no more goal. It ended with 2–1.

Demetrius' team were very happy at their success. They had defeated a very strong team and they were all rejoicing. They could never have imagined the match wouldn't yield any extra time. Just 90 minutes and they had won. The other team felt bad for themselves. They shouldn't have just confronted them. Now, they wouldn't be the best team again because of the cheap bet.

Meanwhile, they kept wondering who the guy that scored the two goals so excellently, was. How he scored the goals effortlessly and finally left with a pain in his leg was surprising to them. They couldn't place their hands on what happened at the football pitch. They began to ask questions as to who he was to their coach, striker and the captain. They wouldn't just accept defeat, if it means buying him to their team, they would be so glad to do it.

"Hey, man." The other team coach called out to Demetrius coach.

"Hey, how far," Demetrius coach said simply as they hugged each other.

"That was a nice one you guys pulled out there. So sad we derided you guys." The coach of the other team said.

"Yeah, we thank God. You guys aren't bad also." Demetrius coach said smiling.

Just then, each of the players began to link up with each other.

"This guy that scored the two goals, who is he?" Jason, the striker of the other team asked Peter who was at that time sitting at the centre of the football pitch looking so confused.

Peter looked up to see him.

"He is our main striker," he said simply, as he wasn't in the mood for any discourse.

The reason they were celebrating was not in the field with them so he could not just see sense in the whole joy.

"I know he is but he doesn't look so normal. Somethings aren't just clear," Jason said, hoping he would get a good response from Peter.

"What do you mean, he doesn't look normal? And why doesn't he look normal?" Peter asked fiercely.

"I am sorry. I meant no harm, I was just saying," Jason said quietly and Peter just signalled to him that everything was alright and he left feeling pissed.

Peter couldn't understand what Demetrius was staring at so he was quite puzzled. He couldn't fathom how he still scored the goal despite his shock and more specifically what had happened to his legs. The thought kept going to and fro in his mind without him getting any answer to it.

In the interim, Demetrius got home immediately to see his granny. As she saw him with that pain, she was so shocked as to what had happened to him. She knew he went for a football match but that wasn't the first time, so why the pain?

"Demetrius, what happened this time?" Granny asked in shock.

"Granny, it's some mysterious being that did this. I don't know why but can you save the questions, please, I am in pain," Demetrius said in pain.

She couldn't bore him with some more questions, so she headed to her room and brought him some healing balm. She placed it on his legs and his legs began to get much better again. He was in so much joy as the pains were all gone. The granny was happier.

"So, tell me, what happened?" the granny asked and he began to explain.

"What's your plan, now," she asked immediately he was done.

"Till I see him again," he said.

As he became well, he just wanted to go back to the school to rejoice with his team. He knew they must have been waiting for him. He couldn't rejoice with them despite that he had scored both goals. He wanted to go but his granny wouldn't allow him to go again.

"Granny, they would be waiting for me. I can't still be here since I am already whole," Demetrius said as he pleaded for her to let him go.

"My child, there is a lot you can do aside from being in the pitch. I really don't want you to be in pain, so can you just forget about that," his granny said quietly.

As his granny said that, he didn't know what to do anymore. He didn't want to argue with her, so he just replied simply with; "Okay, Granny."

Demetrius went to his room to rest from the all-day bustle. He sat back on his bed as he began to think of the devil and the stunt he pulled at the football pitch. He couldn't comprehend how he was the only one who saw the devil. How come he could see both physical and spiritual beings, he tried to fathom but he had to continue in the reality that it was all gone.

As he slept through the night, he thought of his career as a footballer. He loved football so much and he was ready to go further in it. While thinking about it, he slept. God could see through his thoughts and so he came to meet him in the cool of the night.

God came quietly and instructed him not to go deep into the football career. God sat up to tell him that there was more for him to do. He woke up from his bed and began to look through everywhere in his room. He thought he saw someone talk to him physically. He could feel it that the voice he heard was the voice of his father.

"I really want to be a footballer," he said damping the sweat on his face and God came to him physically.

"There is really more you can do, son. You can excel in a greater dimension," God; the father said.

"But, Dad, I am the fastest athlete in this city. Competing with those guys today must have increased my rank in the school and in the society. With that, every club would want to sign me into their team. What do you think?" Demetrius asked passionately.

"You are not just born for the city; you are born for the world; so live by that," God; the Father, said and immediately ascended to his throne.

"So, I have to study something else," Demetrius said and stood up to take action for what he had said.

As much as he loved playing football, he had to head to do something different from his initial plan. Whichever thing he was to do; he knew he was going to excel in it greatly.

He decided to put his mind into something else. He heard of some guys going to the military school. It felt so nice to him and his mind was drawn to it. He told his granny about it and she was indifferent to it but she finally saw sense in it and she allowed him to go.

Demetrius went to his school to tell them of his new exploit. They couldn't comprehend it that he was going to be leaving them for good. The whole school was in disarray especially his team and his teachers. They couldn't believe he was leaving them finally.

Who would win them their gold medals again? They were in fact sad when he said he wasn't going to be a footballer. To them, they felt he was looking track of his vision. How could he prefer to join the army when there was life in football? He helped his whole team with somethings before he finally left them.

"I am really going to miss you all. Just stay good as always," he said as he bid them goodbye.

He went to an army school in the country. He told Peter about his new pursuit. Peter was one of his favourite persons. Peter couldn't still stay in the school anymore since his close friend was leaving. He had to go with him.

Demetrius didn't bother himself so much as to give answers to all the questions his tutor asked him. He went with Peter not looking back to hear what they had to say.

He joined the armed forces finally and started a new life there. He just thought that was the best thing for him to do to please his father. He needed God; the father action in his life.

The first day at the army school with Peter was really stressful but he still did well. He felt he was at home as he got there. It was very different from his former school. Things looked so right and he was ready to stay there forever, since he had no plan for tomorrow.

Months began to meet months and then years. He began to do excellently like always and the soldiers began to prefer him more than any other superintendent or student. There was no stress for him to learn things. In the space of a little time, he had learnt a lot of martial arts and was very skilful at it. He could contend with a host of people without getting hurt. That was the best for him.

He passed through hell and he had to put in a lot of vigour to be able to learn it so well. As a man with a lion heart it was difficult for him to do certain things that the normal human could do but he gave it his whole. He wanted to be the best at everything but he still faced opposition at every realm.

During those recent time, there was to be a battle between the states he was representing and another state. This had occurred several times but it always come out to an unjust end. Many people tended to fight, giving their lives for it. The fight was on again. It was a hectic fight among the people of the states, so it was their armed and most skilful men that came out to fight the battle.

The commander of the team had been observing Demetrius and saw how instrumental he was, so he led him out for the battle. Whether or not he gave his life for it, they weren't so concerned. All they needed were skilled men to meet up with the task for the nation.

The whole army for the Ballistic team which was the team of Demetrius, were all out for war. Everything they were going to be needing for their battle was made available for them. All their swords, shields, guns … were all set and it began to rain bullets.

It was all over the place. The defence was tight and the Ballistic team were winning.

The fight was not supposed to be happening at that time of the year. There was meant to be tranquillity among the soldiers but it was the other states that called for the fight. Pharistinia team; the other team did that which was wrong and were able to seize some of the shoulders of the Ballistic team because they had more armed equipment than the men. That got the whole Ballistic team annoyed as that was never to be done.

More so, that wouldn't have been too bad. It became so bad when the Pharistinia team weren't sorry for their atrocity and they wanted to prove the Ballistic team wrong. They called for the attention of a higher force which they thought were lower than them in the rank. If it was made known to them, that the Ballistic team was stronger than they looked they wouldn't have tried to interfere with their land.

Their men shed their blood for the outrageous fight. No one was backing down from the battle as it was a matter of life or death.

More so, the devil hadn't been able to get over what had happened at the pitch the other day. The devil would never stop in his evil actions till maybe someday it caught up with him. He summoned his major angels to deliberate about the action that should take place. He had seen that Demetrius was well already and that he was into another team. That was a rapid action as that was never to happen. It'd been years but he had been sending people to torment him slowly, now was the time for the devil to strike again.

Demetrius had become so strong and active especially since he was in a strong team. There was no room for laxity and he was very up and doing. To the devil, it didn't matter whether he was skilful in martial arts or not. These wasn't any physical battle but a spiritual one.

He already thought to himself that Demetrius must be a special being sent into the world for a change, but he couldn't place why he was sent to the world. Till that was accomplished, the devil would keep aiming for his life for him to die. The devil most times didn't get to meet him personally.

He had his seeds planted everywhere for attack. This Pharistina team had the indwelling of his children. They didn't just think to themselves to fight against the Ballistic team. It was the devil that hardened their heart and made them choose to fight the ballistic team because he was set to attack Demetrius but what the devil failed to understand was that He that sits in heavenly places, shall laugh.

God in his throne wouldn't just sit back and watch his child die when it is not yet appointed for him to do so.

The devil and his host in the meantime had their meeting in a glass of fire. They sat there as they began to watch the match that was going on among the two strong team.

"Boss, didn't you say you attacked him? See, how alright he is already, what's not clear to us?" The angel of deception asked the devil as they all sat down on a rolling stone.

"The guy is playing with fire." The devil laughed.

"That's him over there." The angel pointed to Demetrius as he was on the battlefield attacking another soldier.

They could see him directly from their coven.

"He hasn't spent so much years with the military force and now he is already in the battlefield, isn't that so strange?" another angel asked.

The devil and his host were all fiercely looking. They had been killing a lot of promising young children just with a fling. It's just so alarming to them that after an attack from them, he was still standing tall. Not just that but that he was in a military team contending with a coup.

"We will launch an attack on him yet again to see what he is up to and from whom his protection is coming from," the devil said smiling in an erotic manner.

"When would that be?" an angel asked.

"Now!" he replied and they all disappeared from their coven to the battlefield where Demetrius was.

The war was going on advent and Demetrius seemed to be surprising all the people as his attacks were right on target. There was no mistake! As he was hitting it, they were falling in a circumspect way on the ground. It was a great defeat.

As the attack was coming to a close end, there was a shot at Demetrius' legs. Immediately, after this shot, he fell straight to the ground. The team were confused as to how one shot could make him fall because he was supposed to be wearing a bulletproof suit all through. When the battle had subsided, they checked his body and saw that the bulletproof suit was still on his body.

"How did the bullet penetrate?" the commander asked.

Immediately as they said this, Demetrius looked towards the end of the field and there at a corner, he saw the black beast which was the devil. Somehow he knew it was going to be the devil, but he couldn't just understand why the devil was bent on taking his life. He thought it was enough for him to make him leave his football team. He didn't think to himself he would still see the devil again after the encounter he had with him.

How did he find his address now that he was in this army, Demetrius wondered?

He was in pain and the devil and his host kept laughing hysterically hoping they would see a being who would come to his rescue. But God was just in heaven looking at their show of shame. He knew how he was going to protect his son, he just wanted them to have their way as he had a counter plan which would amaze humanity.

Demetrius was in so much pain and he needed to go see his granny immediately. The men couldn't understand why. They were talking about taking him to the hospital but he refused them. The head of the army of soldiers made sure he got home safe and sound.

He got home quite on time and his granny was there to heal him of the pain in his legs. She didn't know what else to say to him; either it was a good choice for him to be in the army of soldiers or not. She just healed him of the pain and laid him to rest.

While he rested, God the father came to meet him and comforted him through his sleep.

He got up the next morning feeling so hale and hearty with no form of pain in his bone. He was grateful for yet another life again. It didn't matter the number of injuries he got, he could never die. The pain might be there but in a space of night turning to morning, it would disappear. He didn't know how he had the lion heart and he had no idea why he was being trailed by the devil. The ability for him to see through the four dimensions were all a mystery to him.

He sat on his bed as he began to consider life and humanity. He remembered the words of his father that he wasn't just a person to be known by a city but by a world. He couldn't relate with those words. Though he knew he wasn't a natural man, he didn't know what else he needed to know about his being. He just had this strength none of his contemporaries had.

With the joy in his heart, he went to the barrack. As the captain sighted him from afar, he was amazed at his quick recovery. There was in fact no sign of the scar the bullet had caused, in his legs. He was as agile as before. The captain could not believe how quick his healing had been, so he hit him with the rifle in his hand to be sure of his identity.

As the rifle hit Demetrius, the activation of the first Adam began to showcase in his body. His whole body became so stiff and his eyes began to wander around even as he began to see hidden things about people. He could see the first dimension of sight which was the brown eyes that could sense good people from a distance who aimed to do good to him. This was his first dimension of the eye. As his eyes began to broaden further, he was able to see through his blue eyes, the bad people that were in the life. These bad people knew they were bad and loved doing bad things.

The third dimension he saw was with the green eyes where he was able to see those who are doing bad but they are controlled by the forces of evil nature; they have no intention of doing that which is bad. The fourth dimension was the black with no white eyes where he saw people like angels both the good and the bad angels but majorly the devil.

Demetrius' eyes weren't stable as they began to move through all the dimensions. He began to see through the soul of every man that walked upon the earth. The first Adam named the whole creatures and had dominion over every living thing. Immediately, Demetrius began to gain prominence to every detail about living creatures. His power was activated.

As he stood before the people, his eyes began to change. The captain was dumbfounded at the being before him. He didn't know if it was the Demetrius he was talking to that was in front of him. He was so scared and everyone around became scared.

After some minutes, Demetrius spirit was pacified and he came down to the level of everyone and it appeared unto them like they were thrown into a trance. They couldn't recall what had just happened as he went into the barrack holding the commander by his hands.

He continued staying in the barracks for a long time. Though he had already gotten the powers as another Adam, the devil still tormented him. He couldn't attack the devil because the father hadn't given him the permission to do so. With all that the devil kept doing, his granny was there to heal him of every illness according to the power that was working in him.

There were many challenges he went through in the barrack but he still stood out. The people could not imagine the kind of strength he had whenever he stood out for a war. Yet with the powers and abilities he had, he was still humble to the core. He always gave honour to whom it was due. He was loved by many and hated by the children of the devil.

Their hatred couldn't amount to anything because he was still doing perfectly well. His eyes were the mirror of his soul as he was able to see through everything. Before any danger was to come his way, he usually knew about it and prepared for it. Nothing caught him unaware.

He could also tell of a good person from a distance and get close to them for his benefit. The eyes were his instrument of war. The devil knew he could see him but there was no way he could stop him from sighting him. All of his schemes are usually temporary because towards the next day, Demetrius would have already been perfectly fine like nothing was wrong with him before. He was a terror to the devil and his host of angels.

How was he able to see through many people with just two eyes, the devil always wanted to know? Demetrius had many faces though with the same eyes. He could determine whatever he wanted to see. He had that kind of control of his body that the world could not understand or know how he was doing it. He could change into another form but still with the same body and eyes, just the face would be the constant change.

This he did most times to disguise himself before the bad ones. He would have sighted them from a far distance that they are with an evil scheme. They would have known his face and be aiming towards him but as they were about to get at him, he would change to another face, leaving them clueless.

There were various cases of attacks that they posed at him but he came out triumphant. It's how unstoppable the devil can be to the dealings of man. The devil turned a lot of people away from Demetrius. He started causing people to see fault in him such that whenever it was the appropriate time for him to do any good thing to man, he made him unconscious by breaking his legs. His legs were always the target of the enemy and the enemy never wanted him to do anything good to humanity.

Demetrius was saving a lot of people and still causing a lot of people to be in danger of self and mind. As he was sorting out to protect himself, he knew he had to protect the people around him because when the devil came to attack him, if there was a good person with him, the devil would also attack that good person. Somehow man was always limited in sight, they only saw what happened physically which wasn't enough. There were times a good person might be doing something and the devil was just close by looking for a spot

41

to attack such a person. Since man could not see him, they were in most cases attacked greatly by him, unknowingly.

Demetrius had this passion for men and women and he was willing to save them from the hardship they had brought upon themselves.

He got into some trouble in the military school. He was misjudged for all that he had done some years back. The devil brought into the memory of the people the pursuit of some years back which he was never aware of. With this, he was hopeless as people viewed him differently. No one could relate on how he was living life. He didn't get help from people anymore and he began to suffer to get so many things. At that time, he was 41 years of age. He began to learn and understand things going on spiritually.

Things became so hard for him such that on a particular day he called on all of the devils to face him. He realized that all the black eyes he had were all the image of the devil. They came to meet with him and he began to engage them in life altering conversation.

"Who are you and what business do you have with my life?" Demetrius asked in anger as he was done with their side play.

"You want to know my identity?" the devil asked as he was laughing hysterically.

"Yes, I want to know it. So, just begin to talk," Demetrius said, in confidence.

"Well, if you must know, you can just come to join us in our large palace under the ground," the devil said and all his angels laughed with him.

"This is no joking matter and I am not following you into any ditch, black beast," Demetrius said as he tried to get them angry.

"You know my identity, so why do you ask?" The devil looked at him in anger.

"That's because I don't know why you have been in my life all this year," Demetrius said in anger.

"Well, if you must know, I don't waste time on a person. Once I am done with my mission, I move to the next target," the devil said.

"Have heard enough of you, so you can move now!" Demetrius said expecting them to leave him.

"I can't leave without knowing every information about you and as to where you draw your strength," the devil said still observing him.

"What are you talking about?" Demetrius asked.

"If we couldn't kill you all this while we must find the power that is protecting you from all our evil deeds," The devil said painstakingly.

"If you never find this power, what would you now do to me?" Demetrius asked and the devil signalled to his angels to beat him up.

Demetrius tried to escape as he saw the angels coming near to him. They caught up with him and broke him into pieces. They made sure he was broken till he had no strength in his bones anymore. It was after this they left him lying helpless.

His whole body was broken and he needed healing. He carried his body, squeezing himself to the edge of his walk down and he called on his granny to fix his broken body. His granny as usual held him passionately to her arms and repaired his broken bones.

He got back into his room after he was already made whole. This time he didn't call on the devil, he called on his father.

"Father!!! Where are you?" He cried unto his father several times to give answers to his tears.

Finally, after some minutes, his father appeared unto his midst.

"Why, son? Why did you call me?" God asked, like he had no knowledge of what was going on.

"Father, why do I have this lion heart and why am I in pain all the time?" Demetrius asked his father pathetically.

"It's because you are different, son. You are my own son who I sent to this world to become the last Adam." God explained.

"Last Adam?" he asked.

"Yes, son. I created Adam and his Eve some years back but they defaulted. Since then, the devil has had free access to destroy any man. I sent you to put a stop to his evil acts and that was why I gave you the heart of the lion because that is where the soul of the first Adam is." God continued.

"But, father, he is the one attacking me. How do I put a stop to it?" Demetrius asked?

"He can never kill you no matter how hard he tries. Just keep doing what you are doing by doing good to people, son. Those are just the persecution you are to face for humanity's sake." God explained.

"So, after some years the devil would be appeased." God concluded.

"I will wait," Demetrius said.

"The devil wants to have a conversation with me now. I can sense his atmosphere. I will be back some years later. Let's see what he has to say," God said as he disappeared.

The Mystery

God began to walk unto his throne with the host of angels that followed him. As he was about getting there, the devil beckoned him for a discussion. God already knew he was coming so he wasn't surprised to see him. With his omniscient ability, he knew what he was to say already but since he is God, he still waited for the devil to speak before he said what was in his supernatural mind.

"Yes, how can I help you?" God said as he turned back in his majesty.

"Who is the guy, Demetrius?" the devil asked in mischief.

"Haven't you considered him so well that you know who he is?" God replied.

"All I know about him is that he is not just like every other creation. His heart isn't made with pure flesh but of a lion. I have searched in my watch to see if any of my angels bestowed him with such powers but since there was no one, it is glaring to our eyes that you have his back." The devil lamented.

"So, why are you here?" God asked calmly.

"To know who he is!" The devil replied in shame.

"You said I have his back, so what else do you want to hear!" God asked him.

"You are in control of everything and you protect the ones you love but I destroy the ones you love. I have tried destroying him but he still gets back on his feet that day. It shows there is a great power you have given unto him, which I don't understand." The devil lamented again.

"With all the powers you have, you couldn't just attack him?" God smiled at his almighty self.

"That's because you have put a shield over him and concerning all that concerns him." The devil kept on lamenting.

"So, what do you want me to do about that?" God listened to him.

"Remove this shield from him, I pray, sir." The devil pleaded.

"Whether or not the shield is there, he is still always protected. The only agreement I can make with you is that I wouldn't interfere with his matter anymore and you must not interfere with him anymore. I have my descendants in the earth and you have your descendants in the earth. Let both of our descendants bruise over each other. At the end, we would know who will triumph," God said and was leaving.

"If that is it, I will plant more of my descendants everywhere in the earth," the devil said and left the presence of God.

"It's going to be a battle," the devil said in horror.

God looked from his mightiness and said; "Woe unto the inhabitant of the earth for the devil is come unto you."

As the devil left the presence of God, he summoned all his angels for an important task of immediate and life threatening operation.

They all gathered with their furious faces as they were ready for war. Whenever the devil called for such a meeting, they were sure of it being deadly. They were always ready for any bad assignment. The sorrow of the people was their own joy.

"Yes, boss we are all here." They began to introduce one another.

"I am Lucifer and I operate in the pride of the spirit. Everything in this world is under my control." The devil started and all the others continued.

"I am mammon! The spirit of greed. Men are never satisfied and I make them so!" Another exalted himself.

"I am Asmodeus and I am the spirit of lust. Man would always want more than they have from the other. I am the mystery behind that!"

"I am Leviathan and I am the spirit of envy. Whether or not man has more than enough, they would still feel bad at the success of another. I am that mystery to them."

"I am Beelzebub and I am the spirit of gluttony. I am the vice that make people to eat in excess as their spirit becomes weak because their flesh is filled up."

"I am Belphegor, the spirit of sloth and I am the instrument needed for the operation of today. Lucifer here I am send me," the last angel said.

The devil in his high esteem began to extol himself as they bowed down in reverence to him;

"I am Lucifer! The Abaddon for ruin and destruction, the Armaros, the Amnon, the Satan. Everything and everyone in the earth is at my fingertip," he said and they all bowed in reverence.

"It's good we are all gathered today in the strength of our power." He continued. "Here is the operation we are to do. We need more of our descendants in the earth. The ones we have aren't enough. We have to make our kingdom more populated than the kingdom of God," the devil said in wrath.

"What am I to do?" Belphegor asked.

"You, as angels will mate with the children of men. Whatever time it is, possibly in the night when their soul is weak, you would go up to the women and mate with them. When they conceive, they will give birth to children of our kind." The devil concluded and all of them laughed.

"Why the women?" Asmodeus asked laughing as he knew the answer.

"The first woman on earth was our first target so to the end of the earth, women will always be our target! We must never forget!" the devil said in verbatim.

"We start up today then! Every woman is our target."

They all made allegiance to the devil as they set out to go. The devil sat in the coven as he watched through the earth.

"We are coming for you," he said joyfully.

The earth was ignorant of the plans of the devil, they continued their own sweet life getting married to each other, loving each other and having sexual intercourse with each other. They had no thought of the plan of the devil. There was no one to tell them as God had made the agreement not to interfere in their matters. God just sat in the heavens watching how everything was going.

No matter how hard the devil tried, he knew he can never get smarter than he. He can just try but he can never win.

Man became connected with nature as the whole operation started all over. The devil started his operation so fast. He was so determined of ruling over the world. If this was the only way he had, he was ready to meet up with it to the end of time.

He started with a new set of family. This was a very peaceful family that had just got married. All they were just doing after marriage was fondling, loving, kissing, having sexual intercourse and all, there was nothing so much special than love. They were really happy to be getting married as they really loved each other.

It was another night for the Cokers.

The husband and the wife were having a fun time in their bed as usual, fondling with each other. They had a nice time through the night and finally slept. While they slept, the spirit of sloth; Belphegor crept into their room. They were already fast asleep when he began to open up their bedspread. He looked at the man and laughed out loud but the man couldn't hear him. He immediately began to open up the clothes of the woman and then he started having intercourse with her. She didn't know any such thing was happening as she was so deep in the natural realm. By the time Belphegor was done, he left there excitedly.

"Mission 1 accomplished," he said and finally left.

The woman kept enjoying her sleep then after some minutes she woke up into reality. She could feel that something came into her body but she just couldn't place her hand on it. She kept checking herself thoroughly and that woke Mr Coker up.

"Hey, dear. What is it?" he asked, as he woke into reality.

"I really don't know there but I feel like something entered into me," she said confused.

"Something like what?" he said as he was battling with the sleep in his eyes.

"I really don't know. I was just disturbed," she said feeling puzzled.

"Go back to bed, dear. There is nothing wrong with you. You are perfectly fine," he said and cuddled her to sleep.

As they slept off, the host of the devil began to watch them as they were ignorant of their vices.

After some days, the woman began to feel pain in her belly. She didn't know what was that as she was vomiting circumspectly.

"Are you sure you are fine?" Mr Coker asked as he observed her.

"I don't know. I just need to see the doctor first," Mrs Coker said.

"I hope it is what I am thinking," Mr Coker teased.

"What are you thinking, just don't be too sure. Let's go see the doctor first." Mrs Coker concluded and they went to see the doctor.

Their heart was raised high as the doctor said she was two weeks pregnant. Their soul was so lifted high. They couldn't just stop feeling grateful for each other. Just that, they had no idea that the child in her womb was the child of the devil and that the devil was up for his plan to the earth.

They kept on rejoicing in the earth and the devil kept on rejoicing in the spiritual realm. They continued to plant more seeds in the womb of the women through the earth. Whether or not God liked it, the devil was bent at making the world his own. He just thought to himself that God can keep up with his heavenly place but for this earthly place he was ready to have dominion. He had no thought of who could take his place as he stood at the centre of the earth extoling himself.

In the interim, God kept on doing good with the hands of Demetrius. God was never going to leave his son alone regardless of the devil's scheme. It didn't matter whether or not God was present with Demetrius. What mattered was that Demetrius was covered hitherto he went. Most times, God didn't call him Demetrius but as his son. He knew Demetrius was just the earthly name that could be bestowed on him.

There was a deeper dimension to his name and his abilities. Either the devil was in for the trial or not, it was a battle between good and bad. If the bad would keep winning, God would have to wait to see how far he can go. The creature can in no way be greater than the creator. Never!

The devil anyways still had the chance to attack Demetrius but he was still trying to keep up with his promise of not interfering. The devil however isn't someone to not break promises. Whether it was now or tomorrow, he is definitely going to break his promise. God been so omniscient knew he couldn't just be having a deal with the devil, he just wanted to see how far he can go in his schemes and operation.

However, the devil had tried Demetrius many times and he came to the knowledge that if he should but continue, it might just be a fruitless effort. He knew Demetrius liked doing what was good but he just couldn't relate with why he would choose good over bad. He was still always going to come after him but he had a focus first. His descendants were his priority. He left Demetrius for the time since he was going to continue with his good life for the time being.

Demetrius didn't disappoint the devil's trust of being involved in good things. To him that was what he was born for. It was just good he had started up with it and he had the back up of his father. He was really so glad with the four types of eyes he had.

Sometimes what was needed to fight a battle in all realms was just the ability to see ahead of time. Once he could see evil coming from an angle he could quickly dive to another angle. If he wasn't able to see, the number of troubles he would have fallen into would have been so outrageous.

So, he had the eyesight to see both good and evil but it is so amazing that he chose to do good only. He was never ready to disappoint the lover of his soul. He began to do good in a high and unimaginable way. The power of God was resting upon him but he didn't know in what realm he was manifesting. He just knew he could see beyond the realm of the physical and he could help everyone in need of help. Most times, he tries to analyse how the power came to being in his life and he couldn't just attach it to a particular person.

His life was always a mystery to him but he somehow knew his father was set to do something beyond man's control, out of him. Till he found that, he would not stop aiming at the right core.

He started helping people in need of help from him. His eyesight wasn't just for the benefit of himself alone. He had to extend his watch to other people. Life wasn't to always be one sided. There was no benefit of things if they are just limited to one person. Other people should also benefit.

Demetrius couldn't always hide his eyes from the people. He was sent to the people so he began to help them. Whenever any evil deed was going to happen to any of the children of God, Demetrius would be able to see ahead of time and shield them from such evil. God didn't have to be in a competition with the devil as regards raising offspring. He had enough of them in the earth and he was still producing many. His aim was to just shield them from the hands of the devil because man generally can be so ignorant. Demetrius was in that realm doing what was right by helping the children of men gain sight of their reality and of the enemy's attack.

The devil and his host continued in their evil devices and they were attacking humans in different ways. They were using different schemes man could not understand. To get back at the women, the devil invented new diseases and sent it to the body of the woman. So when any of his angels were having intercourse with them, they were also inflicting diseases on them.

An average woman would just sleep and wake up with pains all over her body. That was the plan of the devil. Each time that happened, the doctor tried to find out what went wrong, the causes and what exactly the illness was. Most of the time, the disease couldn't be traced to any other human but was just there lying faintly in the body of the woman.

The treatment took a lot of time and some time there was no cure to it. The devil hated the woman race and was doing everything to frustrate the woman. Their connection from the beginning of the first Eve and the snake was still dwelling in the devil's heart as he just doesn't change from his evil nature. It's either he was destroying the woman race or he was planting his seed in their body. His attention was just always centred at the woman as he knew they were the reality of life. Life starts from their belly, so he would catch them right from there.

More so, the devil wasn't biased. When he says; destroy! He wasn't selective. He means all. Both male and female.

54

Though, the only thing he was doing to the men was that he was making some of them become impotent. It's so sad how the devil is an expert in all of the evil crimes. He is the father of evil deeds. Every evil operation comes from his throne. An evil man can but just have a glimpse of him, not all of him. He would never reveal the whole of his self to people except if it was extreme.

His evil actions to the men, stopped some of them from getting married. It was somewhat thoughtless for them to find out they can't make a woman pregnant and still go ahead with the marriage. Those who are as evil as the devil could go on with the plan for the marriage without telling their wife their little predicament. They were the likes of people Demetrius saw with his green eyes.

The ones who were upright but just a victim of the evil circumstance could not always continue in their marriage because they couldn't just explain what happened that made them impotent. No woman would want to marry an impotent man as there would be no fun in the marriage. The best the man does is to give excuses for his inability to marry her and for him to continue in the pain of his life all his days. That was the plan of the devil. He doesn't want to ever see any creature happy. Once they are sad, then he can be joyful, but when they are joyful, his sadness would just kick start. With all he was doing, things were not getting any better.

God in his chambers would look down at the earth and feel empathy towards them. He loves mankind so much so all he is doing is looking for the best way to help man. The vessel he is using is still working in the dimensions he can walk in. The earth just had to be patient to see the wonders of the lord before the ends of time.

The devil was indifferent to God's plan as he went about with his angels destroying the world with his evil deeds. He continued with the men for the meantime and he attacked a man by the name Jairus. Jairus was a very upright man enjoying his life in the best of the way. He wasn't doing any bad malpractice. He was just living as a good child of God. The devil noticed him and decided to alter his life. The devil doesn't just target anybody. Sometimes, he goes to the children of God to test how far they can keep up with their good acts or compromise in their faith.

Leviathan attacked Jairus while he was sleeping. Jairus was unaware of their operation. The angel of envy did what he was to do and finally left the presence of Jairus.

Jairus slept and by the time he woke up, he noticed some pain in his public area. He began to scratch his panties repeatedly as he could feel the pain from within. He just thought it was a normal itching that would go in days until it became so frequent that whenever he was with people he wouldn't be able to hide the pain. The devil made it so obvious for Jairus. For some other people, they could become impotent and for several months and years they would have no ideas of it but for Jairus he made the itching consistent for him to know what was wrong with his system.

After persistent effort, he finally resorted to go to the hospital for treatment of the pain as he thought it was just a minor pain where he would be give ointment to use on it and some antibiotics. It wasn't just that. As he told the doctor, the doctor carried out a series of tests on him to prove what he was saying but the doctor couldn't just see a minor pain. The doctor carried out so many other tests on him and it was made known.

"Sir, since when did you start feeling this pain?" the doctor asked as she checked through the test results pathetically.

"Just some days ago," Jairus responded as he watched the doctor reading through the test results again.

"What is the problem, doctor?" he asked.

"I am sorry but, you are impotent," the doctor said directly.

"Im-po-tent! What do you mean by that?" Jairus began to lament as the doctor began to give so many long facts of what could cause impotency.

Jairus' mind wasn't in the speech, he stood up in bewilderment and left the office.

Jairus was dejected. He couldn't imagine what had just happened to him. He was about to get married to the love of his life and this was already happening to him. He was dejected all along and didn't know what to do for him to get better.

His impotency didn't seem like one that could be cured anytime soon. He tried to think of how the illness came to play in his life but he couldn't lay out any fact. He was so depressed as he didn't know what to do with his life anymore. He couldn't tell his supposed fiancé anything about his plight because he knew she would just think to herself that he had been deceiving her all along.

"How can my life degenerate to this level!"

"Impotent, how!"

"From where to where?"

"Oh God, who did this to me?"

"Ah! My life, my marriage, my children, all a mirage!" He cried as he was lamenting all through his house helplessly.

He made up his mind that since God could not save him from his new illness, since he cannot tell his fiancé and there was not going to be any marriage for him, he would just commit suicide. He didn't see any reason why he should still be living. He felt alone in his world as he took up the rope he was going to use to hang himself. The devil was so delighted to see that. What more could he be expecting? Another person was coming to meet him in his realm, he thought.

Jairus, however was on his way to commit suicide when Demetrius found him. Demetrius saw him with his brown eyes so he was able to denote that the man had a good heart. It's how God never forgets his own. It was in no coincidence that he was met by Demetrius but based on God's arrangements.

Meanwhile, Demetrius could see the attack of the devil upon his life. He saw him holding up to a rope in his physical hands but in his spiritual hands he was holding a knife that was filled with blood as he was crying helplessly. Demetrius couldn't waste any more time as he could see that if he doesn't help the man on time, he would be dead in a short time. So, Demetrius set out to help him. He called out to him from his hopeless situation.

"Hey, you! What is it you are trying to do?" Demetrius asked as he went to where he was standing with the rope inclined to his arms.

"What does it look like I am doing?" Jairus said in pain as he began to lament, he really needed someone to talk to or someone who could save him from his situation. "I am done with this kind of life I am living! I just want to end my life." Jairus lamented in pain.

Demetrius could feel the pain in his heart. He knew it wasn't any more normal.

"Not with this kind of good heart," Demetrius said emphatically as he touched his arms calmly.

"Good heart! What do you mean? I don't understand what you are saying?" Jairus tried to calm down.

"I know you are not a bad person. You are just being attacked by the devil. I need you to open up to me, so that I can help you out," Demetrius said painstakingly.

There was no way Demetrius could help him out of his mess unless he opened up in the affairs that had to do with him. Demetrius could just see through but he didn't yet have the power to understand the whole concept and without understanding what was wrong with him, his help to him would be minimal. So, he asked him to tell him what happened to him.

Just about that time, the devil noticed what was happening on earth between Demetrius and Jairus. The devil was so annoyed from where he was seated. He had tuned to watch other things happening in the earth such that he didn't notice when Demetrius started talking to Jairus. The devil could not take chances as he was moved from where he was. In the split of a second, he sent one of his angels to alter their discussion. There needed to be an alteration immediately.

Immediately, his angel flew like a wind and changed himself into a bird. He couldn't just appear in his real identity since it was so urgent hence he disguised as a bird. He began to fly to where they were discussing to change the atmosphere of things.

Demetrius looked up and sighted the bird. As he sighted the bird, his eyes turned black and so he knew it wasn't just a bird but an angel. He held onto Jairus and told him to begin to run with him. Jairus didn't know what to do as he was explaining what was wrong with him. He didn't understand what Demetrius meant by, he should just run. Yet, he couldn't take chances. He began to run with Demetrius helplessly. The bird kept flying with them, not stopping.

Demetrius knew he needed to do something quick as the bird flew faster so he turned unto Jairus and looked at Jairus closely in the eyes. Jairus was so scared at how his gaze changed but as he looked at him every pain in his body began to melt away. He was so confused and didn't know what just happened. As the pains were melting away, the bird stooped on Jairus head. As that happened, Jairus lost consciousness and collapsed.

There was an alteration of powers at the very instance such that Jairus couldn't bear it. He collapsed immediately and the bird looked at him to be sure he was not alive. The angel saw that he was still breathing but he could not do any more harm because Demetrius was there trying to resuscitate him back to life.

Demetrius looked closely at the bird. As their eyes met, the bird looked away. Demetrius stood holding Jairus by the hand and didn't know what to do at that time. Since the angel had done its assignment, he flew back to his coven to give the reports.

"Why is he not dead?" the devil asked the angel like he had no idea of what happened.

"That strange boy was there to his rescue. Anyways he is unconscious now. He should die in his sleep," the angel said.

"That woman is your next agenda. You have to get her fast," the devil said, erasing his mind from that topic.

He pointed to a woman in the earth.

Demetrius held onto Jairus and took him directly home. He was confused as to what to do. Then he met with his grandma. The granny had no insight of what to do to Jairus until he gained consciousness. Jairus was in Demetrius' house for a long time as the impact was really great in his life such that he didn't know what was wrong. Jairus fiancé searched for him throughout the neighbourhood but couldn't find him. She had to accept her fate after staying there for so long a time.

After some days in the belly of his unconscious self, Jairus finally woke up with the help of God from his slumber. God made sure he didn't die in his sleep. Jairus was shocked as to what had happened to him in the last few days. He woke up still feeling pale from the attack of the devil. It was at this time, Demetrius' granny healed him of every disease and he became well. He was so well and his impotence was all gone because of his good acts.

Jairus went on to look for his fiancé and they finally got married. He told her the whole truth and she was aghast at what could have happened if Demetrius didn't come to his rescue.

The devil was not in any way happy as to what just happened. He lost a soul to Demetrius, he couldn't just believe it.

"How could Demetrius heal the person who is doomed for death?" the devil asked himself in anger.

He was in great fury and couldn't forgive himself for what had just happened. He knew there were some mysteries in Demetrius and he was so determined to find them. He made up his mind to frustrate Demetrius till the end and make sure he comes under his feet.

Meanwhile, at that time many of the women he and his angels had intercourse with, gave birth to their children and they all began to grow to become terrors for their parents. The parents tried to find their traits in those children but it was an impossible mission because the devil was the real father of the children. The kingdom of the devil began to populate but his attention was how he was going to find the mystery in Demetrius.

The Son of God

God looked down at the earth and saw how angels had been intimate with humans to form mysterious beings. It resented God in his heart to have created man but he wasn't ready to give up on the man he had created because of the love he had for him and for the plan he had made for his life.

The body of the first Adam was still waiting for manifestation and it was about time the lord revealed his son to the world. God didn't want to do it directly so he gave the devil a chance to still have his scheme as he knew it was but for a short time before his son was going to take over as the rightful heir.

The devil in pain of finding out the mystery behind Demetrius tried all he could but it was always bringing him back to where he had started at. He was just not making progress with the whole work. He decided to involve his angels to the arrest of Demetrius.

Demetrius was with his friend Peter and they were enjoying good old days together but the devil was planning a scheme before him. The devil wanted to gain pre-eminence over him so he stood at his watch as he began to look at him closely to find faults in him. Demetrius was wiser, it was too late for him to do things that were bad so the devil could not track him down with anything.

Demetrius began to teach Peter some of the things he had learnt through the years. Peter stood attentively to listen to him as he was so happy to be in the company of his friend. He left everything he was doing to listen to Demetrius and it was just the best decision he could make. While the devil was scheming out schemes against Peter, it couldn't work because his closest friend was Demetrius. That was but just his saving grace.

The devil came out to have his meeting with his angels as to how to destroy Demetrius.

They stood in their usual way as they paid homage to him.

"Ever at your service, what are we to do next?" Asmodeus asked.

"We need to break him again. See, ever since that guy; Peter has been with Demetrius, we have not been able to get at him. We can't lose yet another member," the devil said.

"At your command, sir." Asmodeus said and headed to where Demetrius and Peter were having a nice time together.

Demetrius saw them as they were coming but he couldn't stop them from doing their evil deeds on him. He only protected his friend; Peter.

Asmodeus began to break him again. To the legs and the hands and Demetrius was in abject pain. He could not fight against the devil that had kept him in such pain. He stood up with the help of Peter and headed to his house. It was a long journey as he walked bit after bit.

The devil could not try to kill him. That was just the only thing he could do to him. He made him pass through hard times. Demetrius could not enjoy his self each time he was in such deep pain and that was but the joy of the devil.

Demetrius finally got home as he held onto his body in pain. His granny who had been upheld by God himself for the protection of his son, took out his healing balm and placed it on his body bit after bit. Demetrius cried as he saw the pain melting away. His tears became like blood because he was angry. He couldn't understand how he could be frustrated by the devil on a daily basis.

He cried to his father that night as soon as he got whole but while he was still about going to his room, Asmodeus came again under the instruction of the devil to break him into pieces. Demetrius whole body shredded into two as the devil cleared off every parts of his body in pain. At this time, his granny took him to the hospital for proper treatment as she held onto his arms applying the healing balm.

His bones needed to be melded, but the doctors could not do anything without carrying out a surgery on him. It was an impossible task as they kept looking at his heart which was not the normal kind of a human heart. The granny kept holding onto him making the pains subside and making the doctor gain stability to heal him. If she wasn't there, the doctor would call it an impossible task.

It was to her glory when he came out feeling better from all the pains. Just in a day and the devil set out two attacks for the son of God. Demetrius was in so much anguish as he walked home still in pain. He could feel and see the evil forces cheering at his pain and at that moment he began to laugh. As he was laughing, they were shocked. They knew he was in pain but the laughter part wasn't something they could relate with. Nothing was of course funny that could be making him laugh.

Demetrius laughed till he got into his house and the devil could not attack him for that day. The devil was bewildered as to how he keeps reforming despite all their evil deeds. He didn't matter to him whoever he is, till his plan comes out to be a reality, he would keep breaking each and every of his organs to pieces. The more God mends it, the more he destroys.

He was ready to see who would eventually win the battle of his life at the end of time. Either, Demetrius dies or the devil dies. The devil said to himself; I cannot die because I am not a human, Demetrius is the human here so he is the one that would eventually die. The devil said it and began to laugh through the days. Is Demetrius a human that could die.

Demetrius had many ups and downs going from one hospital to the other. With the pains he was going through in life, he was not able to live through life in so much pleasure. God in his almightiness released him for the world to see at that time. He allowed him to gain the stardom for the work he was called onto.

His eyes were opened into his reality. Many years back, he activated the power to see the devil and run away from his trap but fortunately for him at that time, he finally saw who he was and his identity to the world. After his long moment with his father pressing him about his life and all he had to do for him not to be subtle to the devil, God came down to expose some realities to him.

How?

"Father, if it is in your own delight, let this cup of suffering pass over me." Demetrius repeatedly cried unto God before God showed up.

God came in his mighty power of wind to meet up with his son.

"Father!!!" Demetrius embraced his presence even as he began to state his matter to the lord.

"Father, the devil has been making a big mess of me despite my ability to see him. How long will this continue for? It's time you raised me up to become the person you have called me to be." Demetrius cried unto the lord that very night when he was back from the hospital with the devil's torment.

"You are my son in whom I am well pleased," God said unto him with so much delight.

"Father, I know I am your son but in what dimension am I called to operate in? These four types of the eyes you have given me isn't just for sightseeing, is it?" he asked rhetorically and God continued listening to him. "I know it should be to gain deeper dimension in the spiritual world and overcome the devil's torment." Demetrius continued and God listened attentively to him as he had grown to such great measure where he understood what was going on.

"The other day I sighted the devil planning an attack on my friend; Peter. I rushed out to help him out of his troubles but the devil came to destroy me. How have I become so weak that the devil can attack me?" Demetrius asked pathetically and God just smiled.

"Father!" Demetrius called out to God as he wanted a response.

"Son, you have grown into this maturity and I am impressed. With this, I believe it the time," God said and smiled.

"You believe? I don't understand, Father," Demetrius said and God smiled again.

"I will make you understand now," God said and began his story.

"Many years ago, I created Adam and Eve. They were my first creation on earth and I really loved them. I showered them with care and attention and made everything under their feet. In love for them, I didn't permit them to eat from a tree because I knew the moment they ate of it, they would be less of a human and less of what I have called them to do. That was the restriction I gave to them." God started and Demetrius listened attentively to the story.

"The devil came around that time and dissuaded my children from what I had told them, he, using the woman as his first target. She fell for his lies and convinced her husband; Adam into believing the lie. They ate of the forbidden fruit and that made them less of a human. I couldn't have them with me anymore, so I threw the body of Adam into the soul of a lion." God paused and looked at him.

"Yes, sir, I am listening," Demetrius said in joy of heart as he was enjoying the story.

"After those years, the devil began to torment man. The man I made to have control over the devil was now controlled by the devil. For many centuries, the devil kept ruling over the man ordering his steps into wrong ways simply because the first Adam and Eve consented to his advice at the beginning of time. I have been looking for a way to bring my people back to me but their soul was so tied up in the devil such that everything he ordered them to do, they did so.

"They couldn't see the devil when he comes up to meet them, they were only led by him. They didn't know when it was the devil leading them into bad things. They didn't know when the devil was set to attack them. They couldn't see the devil because they have lost their sensual eyes with their mistake of Adam at the beginning. As they could not see the devil, they couldn't also see me because they have lost their identity."

"Wow! That's a disadvantage," Demetrius said.

"Yes, son. It is the greatest disadvantage. When man cannot see the mirror of every other soul they begin to live under the shadow of the wicked man," God said in empathy.

"That's so sad. I really can relate with that especially when I seek to help people," Demetrius said in remembrance.

"It's good you can relate. More so, I couldn't just watch the devil keep up with his evil works among my children anymore so I and my angels came up with this plan," God said.

"What plan, Father?" Demetrius asked trying to understand.

"I created the first Adam and Eve and they gave birth to many seeds of the devil. All I needed to do is to create another Adam who would give birth to seeds of my kind!" God said and smiled at Demetrius.

"Wow! That's amazing. So, have you created the other Adam?" Demetrius asked feeling puzzled and God laughed before finally speaking.

"Yes, I created him many years ago. However, I had to set protocols for him to become like me," God said.

"Protocols like what?" Demetrius asked.

"Protocols like allowing him pass through the earth to face the torment of the devil, protocols like allowing a God like himself live like a man, protocols like allowing the son of God be broken by the devil, protocols like providing an angel who he sees as his granny to heal him of all sort of pains, protocols like giving the son of God the ability to see the devil from a distance. Protocols like that," God said and smiled at Demetrius.

As God said those words, Demetrius heart began to move through as he was so shocked.

"Wait, Father. I don't get, am I the second Adam you have sent to the world?" Demetrius asked in shock.

All along he had just been living life enjoying the gift of God. He never had the thought that there was more to the gift of God upon his life. As a son, he thought he was just one of God's special beings who he communicated with, he didn't know it was deeper than he thought.

"Yes, you are the Christ and not just Demetrius. Demetrius is the name the people of the world sees you to bear but in the reality of my operation, you are the Christ sent to this world," God said passionately.

As God was saying those words, the eyes of Demetrius were enlightened, he began to gain more stature in the spirit, his body was overwhelmed, his power was activated, his reality dawned on him and he began to listen to God; his father not like a Demetrius tormented by the devil but as a Christ sent into the world.

"This is why you have the heart of a lion." God continued. "The first Adam was shut in the soul of a lion and that soul was given to you to represent another Adam and destroy the devices of the devil. For so long, have my people been entreated by his evil deeds, now is the time to show him that good would always glory over the bad. So, arise now and make the change the creations are waiting for. The whole of creation is waiting for your manifestation, arise and defeat the world!" God said and the word began to echo in the ears of the new Christ; Demetrius.

"I, Christ shall arise!" he said.

Christ arose in his awesome power to cause about the change in the world. It was never going to be so fast but the years ahead were lesser than the years he had conquered. He was so ready for action but he had to first observe before eventually doing anything.

Meanwhile, at another place in the world the devil continued in his own hassle. You know, he has the dream of conquering the world by attacking the offspring of the woman. He was so pertinent about the Eve of the world so badly. He was so bent on attacking them to the end of time.

The Cokers gave birth to children of the devil and many others gave birth to giants and strange human beings who began to reign on the earth. They began to attack one another and populate the kingdom of darkness. Everything was coming under their shadow and the devil was gaining popularity day after day.

Christ isn't someone to boast. He had to take his victory systematically. He looked at the beginning of the time and saw that the first attack came from the woman; Eve. For him to gain dominion over the world above the devil, he needed to settle the case of the woman. At this time, God began to interfere, since the devil had already broken the agreement as expected.

God called all his angels to his side and had them make a very important decision which was to alter the world. In his chambers were gathered all of his angels as they began to introduce themselves to him.

Gathered together they began;

"I am Cyrus; and I worship you lord."

"I am Seraphum; and I worship you lord."

"I am Metathron, and I worship you lord."

"I am Cherubim, and I worship you lord."

"I am Gadreel, and I worship you lord."

"I am Raguel, and I worship you lord."

The introduction continued as they were all many appearing before the lord at that hour. God finally spoke out after receiving their worship.

"You have done a good job up until now," God said and they all bowed.

"What's the message?" God asked his angels though he knew but he wanted to hear from them.

"Father of light." Raguel began as he addressed God like that. "The devil is keeping up with spreading his offspring through the universe and they are becoming vast. Send your word, Father and we would reorder the world." Raguel said in appraisal of God's power.

"That's not yours to do. That's the work of my son. He would reorder the world but here is why I called you," God said and they listened.

"My son has started a strategy which involves the Eves of the world. You as my angel must pledge allegiance to me as you go out there to mate with the Eves to frustrate the works of the devil," God said authoritatively and they listened calmly, ready to follow his instructions as he brings it.

"From the beginning, I created man and I ensured multiplication. This is going to continue. The seed of the lord must bruise over the seed of the devil. He has formed strange beings to do bad things into the world, you are going to form strange beings that would bring about good to the world. I knew that was going to be his plan so I made that agreement with him and so I allowed him to keep reigning but never again. You as my angels would go to produce the seeds that will mature to destroy the world under the leading of Christ." God concluded.

"At your command, Father." They all bowed.

"You have to be honest and do just good. Nothing more than that, heavenly beings," God said.

"That's duly noted. Your word has come before us and we bow to bring your word to pass. This kingdom will be the kingdom of our God!!!" They all bowed before him singing songs to extol him as they went out to bring to reality what they had just said. It's just but a jiffy when the whole world was going to come to the real end of war.

God sat in his throne and watched the activity of man. He saw the devil and his host going all about impregnating young women. He was effortlessly striving for a position he can never reach.

"Not again, will I allow you gain pre-eminence over my children. It is over," God said as he smiled at the activities going on globally.

Christ began with the women.

The women finally realized they had been the centre of terror by the enemy. They couldn't bear it as they were producing seeds that didn't take after them. The devil was such a terror to humanity as his beings were so strange. There was nothing compared to the human being God had created. They acted strangely and subdued over each other strangely.

The children of the Coker were the worst. They bore more children and all of them were the product of the devil. Night time the devil visited them and began to reproduce his life in the woman. The first pregnancy brought out a giant. He was too big compared to how his parents looked like. The second pregnancy was a miscarriage. The devil was so inhumane to plant a seed and removed it to give it to another woman in desperate need of children.

Years kept eating years, as these children were going. What was it parents wanted from their children, they couldn't get a glimpse from this one. They weren't in any form compared to the creation of God. Man was evolving and the climax of acts was changing but the people remained so blind to the dealing of the devil. They still went to meet some of his contemporaries on the earth to show him love.

That was the devil's greatest joy which they knew nothing of. A woman who had been doing the things of the lord was barren for years. Her marriage was hitting ten years and there was no child to show the fruit for that marriage. She asked of God to give her a child but she didn't get any response from God. She was trying to still believe and hope that God was going to give her a child but it wasn't so like she thought.

Her friends mocked her, the families all around saw her as the reason their son wasn't able to bear a child was all her fault. She couldn't hold on to the insult anymore. She thought to herself that she had tried for the lord by waiting for him and it was the appointed time for her child to wait for her.

What was she to do?

She heard of a man who was into giving people children for them to survive. She didn't care wherever point he was going to get the baby for her. All that mattered to her was she carrying her baby by her hands. She was ready to risk it all. She can't be called barren all over again. She had to do the needful on time.

The devil was a door away from her as he was the one that gave her the baby. All she was just told to do was pay allegiance to the spirit being in the scathed house. She did just that and she was told to head home. It was not long after that she found out she was pregnant and in less than nine months, she conceived her boy. She was so excited that the pain of the years had come to an end. No more would people look at her and call her barren.

However, it would have been better if she had no child than the one she was holding. The child was a direct offspring of the devil and when the devil saw that the woman wanted to go back to the God she had been serving, his son was who he used.

The woman was getting set to dress out to see an expression of God in mankind when this her son came up to her. She thought he was just being protective of a child but he kept repeating with a commanding tone that she wasn't going anywhere. She saw it as some sort of joke and immediately she tried heading out, he pounced on her and choked her to death.

Christ saw that from the position he was seated in his place considering the earth and how he can help the woman race. He saw the death of the woman and was so pained. He couldn't continue with the threat of the evil ones so he drew out for more women to bring them into the light of his reality.

These women began to excel as Amazons to their generation. With the implementation of the angel of God, the children of God began to populate. The children that came out of that intercourse were more mysterious. There knew all the principles that governed the earth and they were operating from the standpoint of goodness and knowledge of God.

These children could see the manifest wonder of the lord and the error the devil was making in creation. None of the children of the devil were attractive to look upon. They all looked like beasts walking in the human form as inhuman. How would they possibly defeat the children of God.

The devil was not aware that God was producing his own seed until he noticed a woman who he had previously had intercourse with, give birth to a child who loved God. That was an alteration of plan. He had to wonder where that was coming from and suddenly he looked up and saw Christ(Demetrius) with some heavenly race helping the woman and some other women from his grip.

He couldn't understand what he just saw as it wasn't so clear.

He was furious!

He went to meet God to ask what was going on with the population. He thought God meant his agreement not to interfere with the dealings of the world, he was really so annoyed to see the world changing bit by bit.

The women began to gain voice again. They couldn't continue through life being blamed for what happened at the garden some years back. That was their mother; Eve but they were different. So, they were willing to fight all evil deeds with every fibre of their being. The theology that reads that women are to blame for what is happening in the world should be erased in their lifetime, they thought. They were ready to live life as an Amazon.

The ability they possessed was far more than what one man possessed and they were far more than the soul of a man. The Eve of this time became brave and pure in heart. They knew they always got the blame for everything that happens in humanity but to them it was a 'not again' operation. The devil wouldn't have his way with them again.

The women saw that the devil operation was usually in the night, so, often time in the night they were awake waiting for the devil to come up to meet them so that they could stop his actions from coming to pass in their life. The devil was losing out on some of his people but not all of them as expected. He wouldn't in anyway give up on whatever happened till the end of time.

However, what he had heard of the controlling factors was enough. He felt so bad that God didn't act like he existed. He was so furious as he called his angels for them to get ready for war. He was ready to fight for the height he aimed at.

He was ready to head out to go meet Christ to attack him. He thought to himself that even if he was being healed of the pain he gets from their evil deeds; he would still crush him over again. If he was still being treated, once he recovered, he would still torture him again. He was ready to do so till Christ got tired of life and gave up.

What he didn't understand was that the Demetrius he knew before had now become Christ. He thought he was dealing with past tense, little wonder it was the present he was dealing with now.

Christ from his position in his spiritual self knew the devil was coming to him with his host of angels. He smiled from where he was, as he waited for the devil to come in to meet him. Christ kept watching all of his activity and his fury all along. Finally, the devil came in to where he was with all of his fiery angels ready for war against him.

The devil came in with full anger ready to destroy and he laughed immediately as he saw Demetrius. He decided to engage him in a chit chat before doing what he is called to do. He saw Christ acting like what he was not.

"Why, how, just tell me?" The devil asked trying to find the best word to use for him.

He looked like someone who wasn't a match for him.

"For what?" Christ asked him as he smiled in fury.

"This kingdom is mine and I gain full access of everything that goes on in it. If you don't know it's best for you to now know. You can't be acting more than yourself; you are a nobody. How will you try to come to spoil what I have started? Do you think I am some sort of joke to you?" The devil asked simultaneously as he was pissed off.

"No." Christ replied simply and the devil laughed.

"What's your confidence today? Is it because you know you will get healed after being broken?" The devil asked and Christ just kept staring at him.

"Demetrius or whatever is your name, it's good to get healing but what you don't understand is that the pain of the moment is higher than the healing gotten afterwards. I will break you yet again and the more you are healed, the more I will break you," the devil said and his angels stood at his back in acknowledgement of his words.

"So, what are you waiting for?" Christ smiled as he talked to them.

The statement made the devil so angry and immediately he began to try to break Christ into pieces. The devil twisted his arms to the left and then to the right, yet nothing happened. He folded his arms yet again as he tried to squeeze his muscles but it wasn't just activating any force of power against Christ. He tried over again yet nothing was done. His angels were confused as to what was going on yet Christ remained on just a spot watching their stage performance.

The devil was getting confused as he checked all around to check if there was any angel shielding Christ from being attacked but he couldn't see anyone.

"What do you think you are trying to do?" The devil asked as he came close to Christ in anger to break his arms but at this time, Christ twisted his arms once and he fell down with all of his angels.

As the devil felt his touch in his arms, he could feel the touch of fire and he didn't know what he was to do. He stood up to confirm what just happened and Christ sent some birds from the heavenly places and it broke some parts of the devil's body. The devil couldn't bear the pain as he immediately vanished from the presence of Christ in shame.

The Victory

The victory of that day was beyond what the devil could think of. He went back to his coven in pain as his angels reactivated him back to his feet after many hours of consistent pain with no results.

The devil finally got on his feet and shouted, "Who is that guy, Demetrius?"

He exclaimed and his eyes began to bring out fire in anger. With the pain in his arms, he went to meet God where God was abiding with the multitude of his angels. He went to inquire from God.

"Who is Demetrius?" The devil asked passively as God glared at him.

"Demetrius?" God grinned. "You are missing it right from the name," God said simply as he doesn't call him Demetrius.

"Whatever name he has, I don't care to know. Who is he?" The devil asked vehemently.

"What do you think?" God replied sharply as he turned on to attend to a whole lot of things in the world.

The devil checked through as he tried to find expression with words in the pain he was feeling and suddenly he saw a host of angels bowing to a being that was clothed in apparels made with the sky. He wondered at who the person was. He knew it wasn't just God they were bowing to because he was still trying to talk to God when he saw the being.

As he broadened his eyes to check further, he looked up to see the mysterious being and there he saw Christ who he knew as Demetrius being highly exalted.

He was dumbfounded as to the whole issue as he spoke out in anger, "Demetrius?"

He was aghast to the whole issue and God answered, "He is no longer Demetrius, he is Christ; my son and the saviour of mankind."

God exalted his son and the devil was so surprised. He just didn't see it coming at all.

"Your son! That's not possible. The heavens didn't celebrate his birth so how can he possibly come into being. I don't in any way believe that," the devil said with all confidence.

"Whether or not you believe it, that's the reality," God said and left the devil staring blankly.

The devil began to think to himself how he met Demetrius. No normal man would be able to see him, the devil, and still be alive. The power he had of the four eyesight were mysterious and the devil looked at the scars on his body. The intensity of how Christ broke him was highly felt such that he knew that for the first time he lost a battle.

That was the first battle for Christ and he won it over the devil. He finally became the Alfa Adam; the black lion as his soul was put into a black lion's body.

After he gained that position in the spirit, he learned it in a hard way and won the first battle with the evil.

The devil kept considering everything he had just heard whether it was some sort of joke or reality. He called his angels to confirm the truth of the word. It was at that point, his angels did necessary research and found out that Demetrius was sent to take away the pains of humanity and set them free from him; the devil's grip.

The devil was not ready to accept defeat.

"Set them free from my grip? That's not possible. It can never happen. Man has been under my control for many centuries now, it can't be now he would stop being under my control," the devil said in so much pride of who he was.

Christ from where he was seated saw how the devil was making a boast of himself and he just laughed.

There was but the last thing, Christ needed to do before he could certify dominion over the devil and the host. Without that, man couldn't be effortlessly free from his grip. There had to be a death to life for man and woman to be saved from the wickedness of man. Christ allowed himself to be broken yet again for the whole of humanity to get the freedom due until his name.

He knew that there was just one way he could open the eyes of man and shut the devil from attacking man again. The trick he used for the first Adam wouldn't always work for him at all and since now there was already a production of good offspring under the work of God, the offspring of God would bruise and triumph over the offspring of the devil.

The devil would try his scheme on man and it wouldn't come to pass as man would have gotten efficient victory over him. It will all start with Christ. So, the devil came again to try Christ to know if he was truly the son of God. He came fully loaded to attack Christ but Christ didn't use any of his powers. He came as a natural man ready to face the wrath of what the people had done.

The devil looked extensively at his eyes with the whole people and didn't in fact know how he never knew that the Demetrius he had been frustrating all along will grow on to become the child of God. Regardless of the truth he had found out about Christ, he wasn't ready to let go.

He believed Christ was the same as he was, after all they were both from God but their mission was just different from each other. He saw Christ coming onto him in the simplest form ready to be broken by him. The devil had no compassion. He saw it was the way to prove his superiority over Christ so while Christ came near, he twisted his arms as he did the last time and Christ's body began to shrink.

Christ became so broken and he didn't go to his granny for treatment that day. The devil was gladdened to see him broken without repairs. The devil thought that was the end to Demetrius and he would now continue doing his bad deeds with no interruption from any good person again.

It was surprising to the devil that after three days of staying in the hospital in pain, he woke up back in health. He didn't need to depend on his granny; who was his personal angel sent by God. His healing came from the indwelling of who he was and he rose, victory was set for humanity.

As Christ came out of the hospital bed in sound health and a stable mind, the first person he sought out to fight was the devil. He needed to gain freedom over him in premium of what he was to do next. The source of victory, Christ was ready to use to win over the devil was the power of sight.

Christ at that point wanted to use his four eyesight to prove to the devil that he was above the world and all of it belonged to him in the goodness of what he was set to do.

Before the devil came to fight with mankind, he saw with his brown eyes the first category of people.

He saw them as helpless angels who had the capacity of doing what was good. His eyes brought them towards his side for support. On the second dimension, he saw with his blue eyes those who were bad and they enjoyed doing the things that were bad. The best way he could save the creature was through the mystery of the sight of the soul of mankind.

When he was about to save someone, if it was the brown eyes that were showing forth, he knew the person meant well and had no bad intention. With that, he could quickly save the person from the trap of the enemy.

The devil tried coming to one of the many children of his in the world, as his brown eyes alighted at the guy, he knew he was bent on doing what was good so he saved him for the purpose of his goodness.

Sometimes, with his willingness to save mankind from the danger ahead of them, his eyes would immediately turn blue. As it activated blue, he didn't bother to go to the person as he could see that the person was willing to do things that were bad. These were the cases of the angels of the devil. They were doing bad and it was in their best interest to keep up with the bad acts. Christ could not help them even as he set them out for destruction.

More so, the green eyes he saw to some people could be so outrageous for him. The ability to keep doing that bad thing because you were being controlled by forces can be so alarming. The only way he could get the person out was when he/she was determined not to be controlled by those forces. Once the person made the decision, immediately, Christ's eyes changed to brown.

Meanwhile, the last stage to the eyesight was the black and not white eyespot as clearly stated. These was basically for the devil and that was how he knew the devil was coming to have a fight with him at that moment.

The devil was loaded for battle but Christ was loaded for victory. The fight started as each party tried to look out who was going to be the winning party.

The fight began with the attack of the devil. He held until Christ and shot many arrows at him. Christ was so resilient as he watched him do all of his evil practices. In just a short time, Christ started with his own fight. He took the devil by his bull and crushed it to the ground. The devil tried to fight Christ at that time but it became so impossible for him. He tried with all of his might but it just did not show. After many hours of the fight between each other, the victory was as said. Christ beat the devil till his bones were broken off.

It was just not so long a time when Christ won over the devil and subdued over the earth. He gained pre-eminence as the head of the earth and all knees came in subjection to his supremacy and being. He gained the victory as the head of the world and the whole earth rejoiced. Nothing could be so much than that.

Christ with all of the experiences he had gotten in life became so pure and powerful like the Lord. While God took his position in the heavens, Christ took his position here on earth as the father. He could not be broken anymore. All he would do was to break the work of the devil and disappoint him from his hiding place.

All of the black witches and wizards that worked for the devil were sent away from the midst of man as they could not cohabit well again with man. The devil's fame began to lower as the lord had all of the victory and honour over the whole universe. The devil could not drag victory with Christ so he stayed in his low corner watching how everything was going to come out and how he would step in. The devil wasn't just a quick nut to crack. Despite the victorious fight against him and Christ, he was still living and planning more evil schemes.

He knew he had been defeated but any chance he got at any human or angel would yield his direct punishment of death or eternal damage to them. He was pained and was ready to take up his life with humanity.

After many years, Christ's body was put into the body of a black lion. The older Adam now began to rule the earth through the proceeding Adam that came in the body of Christ. God was able to get what he wanted for his world. His first creation was restored to the likeness of his son.

Christ began to reign on the earth. He reigned for a long time. After many years of living in a particular land, he travelled to another country to continue to conquer the world. He wasn't just called to a small region but to the main world so he had to move through to enjoy the world in the lord.

More so, towards all those times, he had been talking about love and the whole concept to all of humanity. What God did to humanity was an expression of love and so love had to be displayed everywhere. It was so broad that humanity couldn't stop talking about it. It was evident for all to see that the love of God to the universe made him send his only son to be the saviour of the world. It wasn't something any other person could think of doing.

Christ knew he was always going to reciprocate that love in either ways of life.

And he knew quite well, that true villains would never give up on their life. Even till the end of time, tough people would keep fighting. That was his perspective about the devil. Since the devil cannot die, he knew he had to be up and doing for the devil not to gain prominence over him.

In the interim, Christ travelled around the world and had a girlfriend. These was the lady he loved and she was an offspring of the lord. Christ began to try to do so many works as he grew up learning to do this. As it is known that he has lived his early live as a human. So, he made it realistic again.

The devil was his only obstacle he had especially when he knew that he had been conquered but still living. Christ had a memory of when he had to do everything he wanted to do while living without the knowledge of he; being the son of God but as a person who loved doing good. It was such a memory that made him smile.

Whether or not, he had advanced into a position he didn't bargain for, he didn't stop with his good acts in whatever he did. The only way to rule and to be sustained was to maintain the cores of doing what was right. Christ was indeed goodness and not any other bad traits.

He was never proud even as he was the head of the universe. He still got himself many new friends, in addition to Peter who had been his close friend right from his young age. Most times, he related with the people like he was one of them. There was no seclusion. Peter was so glad to have sustained Christ as his friend all through his life.

Everything Christ did, he was so clever in it and he made a lot from it. He decided to continue to live his life as a normal child and not like some special being. He wanted to relate well with the people he came to the world for hence the reason for his new style of life. He couldn't be far away and expect them to know him as Christ. He called them close. Even for the children, he didn't refrain them from coming close to him.

In the riches of his power, he had so many assets to his name.

Meanwhile, he loved Angela, his girlfriend, so much that he finally got married to her. It was a beautiful marriage. He had talked people into the whole essence of love and he knew love to the opposite gender wasn't just to be casual but intentional. Once the feeling has started for long, it should end at marriage, nothing more. No lust, but love.

The devil, in the hospital, saw Christ start a new life. He was so shocked. It affected him so much to see so many strange things that Christ was doing. He never expected it from him. He thought the Christ he knew about was just going to be so holy without touching anything of the world. The devil didn't know he was so mistaken. Everything that was in the world was for the pleasure of those living in the world. Love is above the world and so Christ himself must show love. Whatever the devil thought wasn't of any sense to Christ.

However, the devil saw it as the ability for him to strike at Christ.

He said to himself one day at the hospital, "If I couldn't get him when he was so holy, I should be able to get him now that he is corrupted with the affairs of the world," in happiness.

The devil was so intent of winning the battle of the world at all cost. That was what he was living for but that didn't seem like a dream that was ever going to come true.

Christ in his chambers heard what the devil said and just laughed.

"I really thought he would have changed with the whole stroke to his bones. Anyways, let him come around to test of my holiness capacity," Christ said smiling.

Christ from his chamber went to meet with his ever loving Angela. He always thought about her all the time and her love made him rule so well. Angela also enjoyed the love Christ showered on her specially. She always counted it as a privilege to have Christ love her to the extent of getting married to her. She was the most favoured of all women.

Together that night, they had a sweet moment with each other in bed. After some days, Angela found out she was pregnant. It came like a shock to her. She was feeling dizzy and Christ came to erase her dizziness, later she began to spill out what she had eaten concurrently. Christ came and healed her. It came over again and that was when Christ inquired from himself what had happened. It was then he found out that she was pregnant.

There was no greater joy than that even as Christ and Angela began to rejoice with each other. The devil saw them rejoicing and right from where he was in the hospital, he threw an arrow in the womb of Angela and she lost the baby. Christ saw it coming but he couldn't stop it because it was in the will of his father for that to happen.

Christ wept bitterly.

Angela felt bad for the miscarriage. She thought to herself that perhaps the whole issue came from her. She apologised to Christ for the miscarriage but Christ just held her to himself and said; it is well. He knew it was never her fault and he was never going to make his woman feel unloved for any moment.

The devil saw them come together and he was pained. He devised for another means. Angela got pregnant again and the same thing happened. The devil visited. It happened again for the third, fourth and fifth time. She continued having those miscarriages.

Angela felt so derailed but Christ comforted her.

They had to visit many hospitals to test out what was wrong with the miscarriages. Christ made doctors and gave them the ability to carry out surgical operation on people and be successful. He knew he could heal people of all diseases but he wanted the works to go round. Only he can't just be doing everything while his own children would be left idle. That was primarily the reason of visiting the hospital. He wanted his children to be able to cure many infections. However, the case of the miscarriages was different. It was more than the scope of the doctors so they just couldn't find solutions to it.

Christ irrespective of the whole bustle got a new house with the assets he had acquired. Nothing was ever going to take his joy. Since that was the will of God he wasn't ready to oppose that. He was going to follow the leading of the lord to the end.

Meanwhile, on the day of the launching of his house, he called a priest to come bless the house. As the priest blessed the house, he prayed for them to conceive and bear children. Christ was the best personality the universe had. He as a God could just bless his house and everything was going to be alright but he chose to leave it for the priest to do so he could hear people exalt the name of God in their respective ways.

After the priest left, when it was night time, he had a nice time with his wife; Angela for them to celebrate their new house.

After some months, God saw it as the time to prove the devil wrong. God finally hid the baby in the womb of Angela at the cool of the night. She was so happy but scared.

"I don't know if I am to be happy with this pregnancy." She said to Christ when they found out.

"Sweetheart, nothing should take your joy. You have to believe in God all time whether or not it comes through." Christ explained.

"OH yeah, I believe in God." She said joyfully.

"Anyways, I am glad to tell you that this baby would stay in your womb and you would conceive it." Christ said smiling.

"Hmm…I believe. But, how do you know?" She inquired as she was glad to hear that.

"My name Christ is a six letter word. This is the sixth time of your pregnancy and it's the end of any miscarriage. This child will come out." Christ said joyously and she embraced him.

When it was time to conceive, the devil tried to attack again. She tried to conceive but it went through so many complications. In fact, the buzzle of it landed him in the police cell. He ran away from there but they the devil came and broke his body in pieces. It was devastating, yet the wife was still in the hospital.

With the pains in his body, the devil took him to an herbalist house to fix his body condition but Christ can never be backward. He is always ahead of the devil. So, with the grace and power in his life he survived and woke up to the surprise of the people. He knew the devil's plan all along so he had to use himself as a game to be played on. The devil lost attention on his wife conceiving and focused on him. He didn't know Christ was not broken, Christ only pretended so he could finally destroy the devil and his host and then save his wife's children.

As Christ woke, he destroyed the devil and all the people that planned against him and he finally came out as a victor.

Not one of his adversaries was left untouched. Everyone hailed him over his victory as he was so powerful. His wife finally gave birth to two children. He called one David and the other Emily. He lived life as a reformed Adam, his wife lived life as a reformed Eve who was pure and brave and together they gave birth to two children who grew up to do great things for the Kingdom. Together as a family, they attacked the bondage of hell and the devil to his last depth.

God was happy to see the reality of his world had been fulfilled in the life of his son. Eve was finally happy that she could no longer be blamed for the mistake that was done anymore as she was a good helpmate to her husband. She never turned his heart from the instructions of God. The load of a bad family was not on her head anymore.

With the heart of Adam and the heart of the Eve finally restored, they were able to fight against the devil and the devil was finally defeated never to appear again. The whole family finally defeated the devil and at the end of time, Christ went to meet his father in heaven.

Christ was reunited with God as one big person in eternity. They now live side by side in eternity as they look at how it all started and how it ended.

Indeed, no matter how long the bad can surface, the good would still always prevail and gain control over the world again.